Reading about animals to your little one can be a fun & educational experience. Here are a few tips for making the most of it:

- **Start with familiar animals**: Show your baby pictures of animals they know, like a cat or a dog. Encourage them to point to the picture and say the name of the animal.

- **Use animal sounds and gestures**: Make the sound of each animal and encourage your baby to repeat the sound after you. This will help them associate the sound with the animal and its name.

- **Point out their characteristics**: Point out the distinctive features of each animal, such as the stripes on a zebra or the wings on a bird. This will help your baby learn to recognize different animals by their unique features.

- **Put them in context**: Describe where these animals live, such as deep in the ocean or high up in trees, or their size, whether they are large or small.

- **Read this book regularly**: Make reading a regular part of your routine. The more often you read it, the more animals your baby will learn and remember.

Remember to be patient and keep it fun for your baby. The goal is to encourage a love of learning and language, not to stress them out or make them feel like they are being tested.

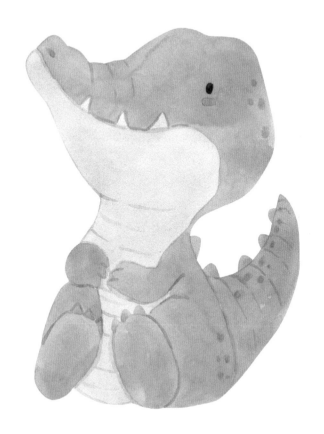

alligator

악어

ag-eo

bear

곰
gom

fox

여우

yeo-u

elephant

코끼리

ko-kki-li

dog

개

gae

cat

고양이

go-yang-i

pig

돼지

dwae-ji

giraffe

기린
gi-lin

hedgehog

고슴도치
go-seum-do-chi

koala

코알라
ko-al-la

lion

사자

sa-ja

mouse

쥐

jwi

owl

올빼미
ol-ppae-mi

rabbit

토끼

to-kki

whale

고래

go-lae

turtle

거북이
geo-bug-i

jellyfish

해파리
hae-pa-li

iguana

이구아나

i-gu-a-na

penguin

펭귄
peng-gwin

snail

달팽이
dal-paeng-i

fish

물고기
mul-go-gi

zebra

얼룩말
eol-lug-mal

squirrel

다람쥐
da-lam-jwi

tiger

호랑이

ho-lang-i

bird

새

sae

goat

염소

yeom-so

walrus

바다 코끼리

ba-da ko-kki-li

narwhal

일각고래

il-gag-go-lae

quail

메추라기
me-chu-la-gi

jaguar

재규어
jae-gyu-eo

yak

야크
ya-keu

reindeer

순록

sun-log

chameleon

카멜레온
ka-mel-le-on

badger

오소리

o-so-li

Find additional Korean & English bilingual picture books on Amazon

Count to Ten in Korean
Learn to count from one to ten with adorable illustrations of animals, flowers, and other fun objects.

People Doing Things
Explore the simple acts of everyday life from eating ice cream to riding a bike.

Did you enjoy this book?
Positive reviews from wonderful customers like you help other parents feel confident about choosing this book. Sharing your experience on Amazon will be greatly appreciated!

Made in the USA
Las Vegas, NV
26 November 2024

12675550R10026